To Dixie and a ripple-free recovery
—S.J.M.

To Thor
—S.W.

HarperCollins®, 🐛®, and MathStart® are registered trademarks of HarperCollins Publishers.
For more information about the MathStart series, write to HarperCollins Children's Books,
10 East 53rd Street, New York, NY 10022.

Bugs incorporated in the MathStart series design were painted by Jon Buller.

ROOM FOR RIPLEY
Text copyright © 1999 by Stuart J. Murphy
Illustrations copyright © 1999 by Sylvie Wickstrom
Printed in the U.S.A. All rights reserved.
Visit our web site at http://www.harperchildrens.com

Library of Congress Cataloging-in-Publication Data
Murphy, Stuart J., date
    Room for Ripley / by Stuart J. Murphy ; illustrated by Sylvie Wickstrom.
        p.   cm. — (MathStart)
    "Capacity, level 3."
    Summary: Uses a story about a young boy who is getting a fish bowl ready for his new
pet to introduce various units of liquid measure.
    ISBN 0-06-027620-7. — ISBN 0-06-027621-5 (lib. bdg.). — ISBN 0-06-446724-4 (pbk.)
    1. Volume (Cubic content)—Juvenile literature.   [1. Volume (Cubic content)   2. Liquids—
Measurement.]   I. Wickstrom, Sylvie, ill.
II. Title.   III. Series.
QA465.M86   1999   98-26109
530.8—dc21   CIP
                                                                                                                        AC

Typography by Elynn Cohen
1   2   3   4   5   6   7   8   9   10
❖
First Edition

Carlos visited the fish at Mr. Peterson's pet store every day. The quick little guppy was his favorite. He made so many ripples when he flashed through the water that Carlos called him Ripley. He would watch Ripley until Ana, his sister, said they had to leave.

Carlos wanted to buy Ripley with his allowance. "First you'll need to make a good home for your fish," said Ana.

She found her old fish bowl in the attic. "I used to have fish myself. I can teach you all about them," she said. "Put some water in the bowl and let it sit for a while. The water needs to be room temperature."

Carlos ran to the kitchen, got a measuring cup, and filled it with water. Then he poured it into the bowl. He knew he would need lots more.

1 CUP

9

Carlos emptied another
cup of water into the bowl.
Now it held a pint of water.

He tried to picture Ripley
swimming around. A pint
didn't look like nearly enough.

2 CUPS

equal

1 PINT

Ana found a bag of gravel, some seashells, and a little blue castle. Carlos dumped some gravel into the bowl. Then he carefully placed the castle in the gravel.

"The water doesn't even reach the top of the castle," said Ana.

"Don't worry, I'm going to add some more," said Carlos.

Carlos added two more cups—another pint. Now there was a quart of water in the bowl. "That's double the water we had before. Now the whole castle is underwater," said Carlos.